AESOP'S FABLES

FAVORITE
AESOP'S
FABLES

Adapted by
Ronne Randall
Illustrated by
Louise Gardner

p

This is a Parragon Publishing book
This edition published in 2003
Parragon Publishing, Queen Street House,
4 Queen Street, Bath BA1 1HE, UK

Copyright © Parragon 2001

Created and produced by
The Complete Works

ISBN 0-75259-844-9

Printed in China

CONTENTS

This book belongs to...

....

AESOP'S FABLES

CITY MOUSE AND COUNTRY MOUSE

Once there was a roly-poly, wiggly-whiskered mouse, who lived in a snug little nest under an oak tree.

Welcome

Country Mouse loved his home. He had plenty of acorns, nuts, and berries to eat, and a warm and cozy straw bed to sleep in.

Squirrel and Robin, who lived in the oak tree, were the best neighbors he could ever wish for.

One day, Country Mouse had a
surprise. His cousin, City Mouse,
had come to visit.

City Mouse was sleek and slender,
with a smooth, shiny coat. His whiskers
were trimmed and elegant.

Country Mouse felt a little ordinary beside him. But he didn't mind. All he wanted to do was make City Mouse feel welcome.

"Are you hungry, Cousin?" he asked. "Come and have some supper!"

But City Mouse didn't like the acorns and blackberries that Country Mouse gave him to eat. They were tough and sour.

Home Sweet Home

And City Mouse thought his cousin's friends were boring.

The straw bed that he slept in
that night was so rough and scratchy
that he didn't sleep a wink!

The next day, City Mouse said, "Come to the Big City with me, Cousin. It's so much more exciting than the country! I live in a grand house, eat delicious food, and have exciting adventures. Come with me and see what you've been missing!"

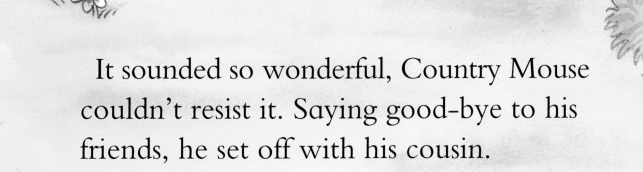

It sounded so wonderful, Country Mouse
couldn't resist it. Saying good-bye to his
friends, he set off with his cousin.

When they arrived in the Big City, Country Mouse was frightened. It was *so* noisy—horns blared and wheels clattered all around them. Huge trucks roared and rumbled down the street, and the smelly, smoky air made the mice choke and cough.

And there were dogs *everywhere!*

At last, they arrived safely
at City Mouse's house.

It was very grand, just as
City Mouse had said. But
it was *so* big!

Country Mouse was afraid
that he would get lost!

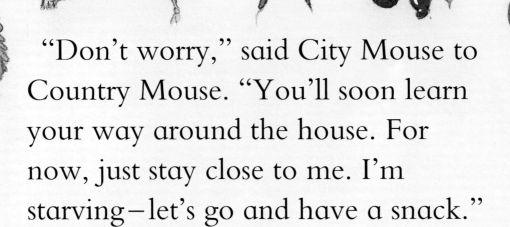

"Don't worry," said City Mouse to Country Mouse. "You'll soon learn your way around the house. For now, just stay close to me. I'm starving—let's go and have a snack."

Country Mouse was hungry, too, so he followed his cousin to the kitchen.

Country Mouse had never seen so much delicious food—there were plates full of fruit, nuts, cheese, and cakes.

He and his cousin ate and ate and ate!

But Country Mouse wasn't used to
this sort of rich food. Before he knew
it, his tummy was aching.

Suddenly, a huge woman came into the room.

"Eek! Mice!" she screamed

She grabbed a big broom and began to swat the mice, who scampered off as fast as they could.

As the two mice scurried across the floor, Country Mouse thought things couldn't possibly get worse. But how wrong he was!

A big cat suddenly sprang out from behind a chair! With a loud

M-E-E-O-O-W-W,

he pounced on the two little mice.

Country Mouse had never been so
frightened. He darted and dashed as
fast as his aching tummy would let him.

The two mice jumped through a mousehole and were safe at last in City Mouse's house.

"Phew! I think we've done enough for one day," said City Mouse, when they had caught their breath.

"Let's get some sleep," he said, with a yawn. "I'll show you the rest of the house in the morning."

Country Mouse curled up in the hard little bed. But he was too frightened and unhappy to sleep. As he listened to his cousin snore, he tried hard not to cry.

The next morning, City Mouse was ready for more adventures, but Country Mouse had had more than enough.

"Thank you for inviting me," he told his cousin, "but I have seen all I want to see of the Big City. It is too big and noisy and dirty—and too full of danger for me. I want to go back to my quiet, peaceful home in the country."

So Country Mouse went back to his snug, cozy home under the oak tree. He had never been so happy to see his friends—and they wanted to hear all about his adventures.

Country Mouse was pleased to tell
them everything that had happened in
the Big City—but he ***never, ever***
went back there again!

AESOP'S FABLES

THE HARE AND THE TORTOISE

Hare was the most boastful animal in the whole forest.

One fine, sunny morning, he was trotting down the forest path singing, "I'm handsome and clever and the fastest hare ever! There's no one as splendid as me!"

Hedgehog, Mouse, and Squirrel
watched him from a fallen log.

"Hare is so annoying," said Hedgehog.
"Someone should find a way to stop him
from boasting all the time!"

"I'll get him to stop!" said Squirrel, and he jumped onto the path right in front of Hare. "I'm as handsome as you are, Hare," he said. "Look at my big bushy tail."

"It's not as handsome as my fluffy white tail and my long silky ears!" boasted Hare.

"Well, I'm as smart as you are!" said Mouse, hurrying out to join them. "I can dig holes under trees and store enough nuts and seeds to last all winter!"

"That's nothing!" said Hare. "In the winter, I can change my coat to white, so that I can hide in the snow!"

"Now, is there anyone who thinks they can run as *fast* as me?" said Hare to the animals who had gathered around him. "Who wants to race?"

No one said anything! All the animals knew that Hare was *very fast*, and no one thought they could beat him.

"**Ha!**" exclaimed Hare. "That proves it! I'm the handsomest, the smartest, *and* the fastest."

"Excuse me," said a small voice.

"Yes?" said Hare, turning around.

"I will race you," said Tortoise.

"YOU?" said Hare in amazement. "The slowest, clumsiest animal on four legs?"

"Yes," said Tortoise quietly. "I will race you."

The other animals gasped, and Hare roared with laughter.

"Will you race me to the willow tree?" Hare asked Tortoise.

"Yes," said Tortoise.

"Will you race past the willow tree, to the stream?" asked Hare.

"Yes, I will," said Tortoise.

"Will you race past the willow tree, past the stream, and all the way to the old oak tree?" asked Hare.

"Of course I will," said Tortoise.

"Fine," said Hare. "We'll start at nine o'clock in the morning! We'll meet right here, at the big oak tree."

"All right," said Tortoise.

The other animals ran off to tell their friends the news.

The next morning, the forest was buzzing with excitement. Everyone had turned out to watch the big race. Some were at the starting line, and others were going to the finish line, to see who would get there first.

START

FINISH

44

Magpie called,
"Ready, set, GO!"

STAR

And Tortoise and
Hare were off!

45

Hare shot
past Tortoise
and the crowds,
and when there was
no one to show off for, he
slowed down just a little.
He reached the willow
tree and looked behind
him – Tortoise was
not in sight!

"It will take him ages just to catch up to me," Hare thought. "I don't need to hurry. I may as well stop and rest."

He sat down under the willow tree and closed his eyes. In minutes, he was fast asleep.

47

Meanwhile, Tortoise just plodded on.

He didn't try to go faster than he could, but he didn't stop, either. He just kept going, one foot in front of the other, on and on and on.

The sun climbed higher in the sky, and Tortoise felt hot.

But he still kept going. His stubby legs were beginning to ache, but he knew he mustn't stop.

Hare just kept snoring under
the willow tree.

Some time later, Tortoise reached Hare, who was still fast asleep.

At first Tortoise thought he should wake Hare up. Then he changed his mind.

"Hare is very smart," he told himself. "He must have a reason for sleeping. He would only be angry if I woke him up!"

So Tortoise left Hare sleeping under the tree and went on his way, one foot in front of the other, walking slowly toward the finish line.

Later that afternoon, as the sun began to sink and the air grew chilly, Hare awoke with a start.

"The race!" he thought. "I *have* to finish the race!"

He looked around to see if Tortoise was nearby. There was no sign of him.

"Hah!" said Hare. "He still hasn't caught up with me. So there's no need to hurry."

And he trotted toward the clearing with a big grin on his face.

When he neared the finish line, Hare could hear cheers and clapping.

"They must be able to see me coming," he thought.

But as he got closer, he saw the real reason for all the noise, and his heart sank.

FINISH

There was Tortoise, crossing the line.
Tortoise had won!
The animals were cheering wildly.

As Hare crept up to the finish line,
the cheers turned to laughter.
His ears turned bright red and drooped
with embarrassment.

Hare moped off, and everyone gathered around to congratulate Tortoise, who looked shy, but very proud. He had proved that slow but steady always wins the race.

The animals smiled at
one another. Somehow
they knew that they
wouldn't have to listen to
Hare's loud, annoying
boasting anymore!

AESOP'S FABLES

THE ANT AND THE GRASSHOPPER

Grasshopper was a lively, happy insect, who didn't have a care in the world. He spent the long summer days relaxing in the sunshine or bouncing and dancing through the grass.

"Come and play!"

he said to Bee one day.

"I'd love to," said Bee, "but I'm *much* too busy. If I don't gather this pollen, we bees won't be able to make honey. Then, when winter comes, we'll have nothing to eat."

"Well, work if you want to," said Grasshopper. "But *I'd* rather play!"

And off he hopped.

Then Grasshopper saw Ladybug crawling along a leaf.

"Come and play!"

he called.

"Sorry, Grasshopper, not today," replied Ladybug. "I'm looking after the roses. They depend on us to guard them from aphids!"

"Well, I think you're silly to spend this beautiful day working!" said Grasshopper, hopping away.

Grasshopper went happily on his way, until he saw Ant, who was struggling to carry some grain on her back.

"Why are you working so hard?" asked Grasshopper. "It's such a sunny day! **Come and play!**"

"I have no time, Grasshopper," said Ant. "I have to take this grain back to my nest, so that my family and I have enough food when winter comes. Have you built your nest yet?"

"Nest?" laughed Grasshopper. "Who needs a nest when life in the great outdoors is *so* wonderful? And there's plenty of food—why should I worry?" And off he hopped.

At night, while the other insects slept, Grasshopper sang and danced in the moonlight.

"Come and play!"

he called to Spider, who was the only one awake.

"Sorry, Grasshopper," said Spider.
"I have a web to spin. Can't stop now!"

"Suit yourself!" said Grasshopper,
as he danced away.

Day after day, Grasshopper played while the other insects worked.

And night after night, he danced and sang while the others tried to sleep. The other insects were angry.

"Stop that noise!"

shouted Bee one night. "You're keeping the whole hive awake!"

"Yes, be quiet!"

said Ladybug.

"I'm trying to get my babies to sleep!" cried Ant.

As the summer went on, the long, sunny days began to get shorter and cooler. But lazy Grasshopper hardly noticed. He was still too busy enjoying himself.

One day, Grasshopper saw Ant with her four little children. They were all carrying food back to their nest.

"My, look at all your helpers," said Grasshopper.

"Well, we're running out of time," puffed Ant. "What are you doing about building a nest and storing food for the winter?"

"Oh, I can't be bothered," said Grasshopper. "There's lots of food around now, so why worry?"

The days passed quickly, and it wasn't long before Grasshopper saw Bee again, buzzing busily around the flowers. Her legs were covered with yellow pollen.

"You're in a hurry," said Grasshopper.

"I certainly am," buzzed Bee. "I have to bring more pollen back to the hive while I can still get it. Summer won't last forever, you know!"

"I don't know what everyone's so worried about!" said Grasshopper. And off he went, leaving Bee to buzz back to her hive.

That night, there was a chill in the air, and Grasshopper didn't feel like dancing.

"Maybe you'd better start getting ready for winter," warned Spider.

It was getting colder, but Grasshopper didn't want to think about that now.

"There's still *loads* of time for that!"
said Grasshopper, and he began to sing.

Soon the trees began to lose their leaves. Grasshopper was spending less time having fun and more time looking for food, but there wasn't much food to be found.

One afternoon, Ant and her children scurried across his path, each carrying a fat, ripe seed.

"Where did you find those?" asked Grasshopper eagerly. "Are there any more?"

"There are plenty over there," said Ant, pointing. "When are you going to make a nest? Winter will be here soon!"

"I'm too hungry to think about that now," said Grasshopper, rushing toward the seeds and gobbling down as many as he could.

A few days later, it began to snow.

Ladybug was in her nest, fast asleep.

Bee was in her hive, sipping sweet honey with her family and friends.

Grasshopper was cold and all alone.
He was hungry, and there wasn't a crumb
of food to be found anywhere!

Spider looked down from his web.
"What are you going to do now?" he asked.

It began to snow harder. "I know," said Grasshopper. "Ant will help me. She has plenty of food."

So he set off to look for Ant's nest.

Once, a blackbird swooped down and almost caught him, but Grasshopper managed to duck out of its way. Now he was cold, hungry, and frightened, too.

At last, Grasshopper found Ant's cozy nest, safe and warm below the ground.

Ant came out to see him. "What do you want?" she asked.

"Please, Ant," said Grasshopper, "do you have any food to spare?"

Ant looked at him. "All summer long, while my family and I worked hard to gather food and prepare our nest, what did you do?"

"I played and had fun, of course," said Grasshopper. "That's what summer is for!"

ZZZZZZ

"Well, you were wrong, weren't you?" said Ant. "If you play all summer, then you must go hungry all winter."

"Yes," said Grasshopper sadly, as a tiny tear fell from the corner of his eye. "I have learned my lesson now. I just hope it isn't too late!"

Ant's heart softened. "Okay, come on in," she said. "I'll find some food for you."

Grasshopper gratefully crawled into the warm nest, where Ant and her family shared their food with him.

By the time spring came, Grasshopper was fat and fit and ready to start building a nest of his very own!